To: Kate and Nathan
Love,
Grace

First U.S. Edition

ISBN 0-316-37647-7

Library of Congress Catalog Card Number 94-79057

Simultaneously published in Great Britain in 1995 by Orion
Children's Books, Orion House, 5 Upper St Martin's Lane, London
WC2H 9EA, England, and in Canada by Little, Brown & Company
(Canada) Limited

10 9 8 7 6 5 4 3 2 1

Printed in Italy

Quacky Duck

Paul and Emma Rogers

Illustrated by Barbara Mullarney Wright

Little, Brown and Company
Boston   New York   Toronto   London

Once upon a pond there lived a duck who was very fond of quacking.

She quacked
at the tractor.

quack!

She quacked
at the cat.

quack!

She quacked
at the farmer's
funny old hat.

She quacked
at the heron.

quack!

She quacked at the fly.

quack!

She quacked at the drake who went waddling by.

She quacked at the clouds.
She quacked at the sun.

She quacked at everything
and everyone.

For when she quacked, she was happy.

And when she was happy, she quacked.

"Quiet please!" begged Dragonfly.
"Quack!" said Duck. "Quack! Quack!"
Dragonfly darted off over the pond.

"Can't we have a little peace?" complained Frog.
"Quack!" said Duck. "Quack! Quack! Quack!"
Frog flopped into the pond.

"Just a day of silence?"
pleaded Very Old Goldfish.
"Quack!" said Duck. "Quack! Quack!
Quack! Quack! Quack! Quack! Quack!"
Very Old Goldfish dived down to the depths
of the pond.

Duck didn't stop quacking until it was night.
Then she went paddling off into the cattails.

The next morning on the pond, something was different. The flies buzzed, the reeds whispered – but there was no quacking.
Duck had disappeared!

"Ah, that's better!"
said Very Old Goldfish.

"What lovely silence!"
said Dragonfly.

"Peace at last!" said Frog.

For four whole weeks Duck was nowhere to be seen.
"It's awfully quiet without her," said Dragonfly.
"It's not the same," said Very Old Goldfish.
"A little *too* peaceful," said Frog.

Then – one lazy, hazy afternoon, when Very Old Goldfish was sunning himself in the shallows, and Frog was snoozing on a log, and Dragonfly was zipping among the shadows – there was a rustling in the cattails.

"QUACK!" cried Duck.

Ten little ducklings hurried out.

"Aha!" said the heron.
"She's back!" said the cat.

"Well," said the farmer,
"just look at that!"

And everyone lived quackily ever after.